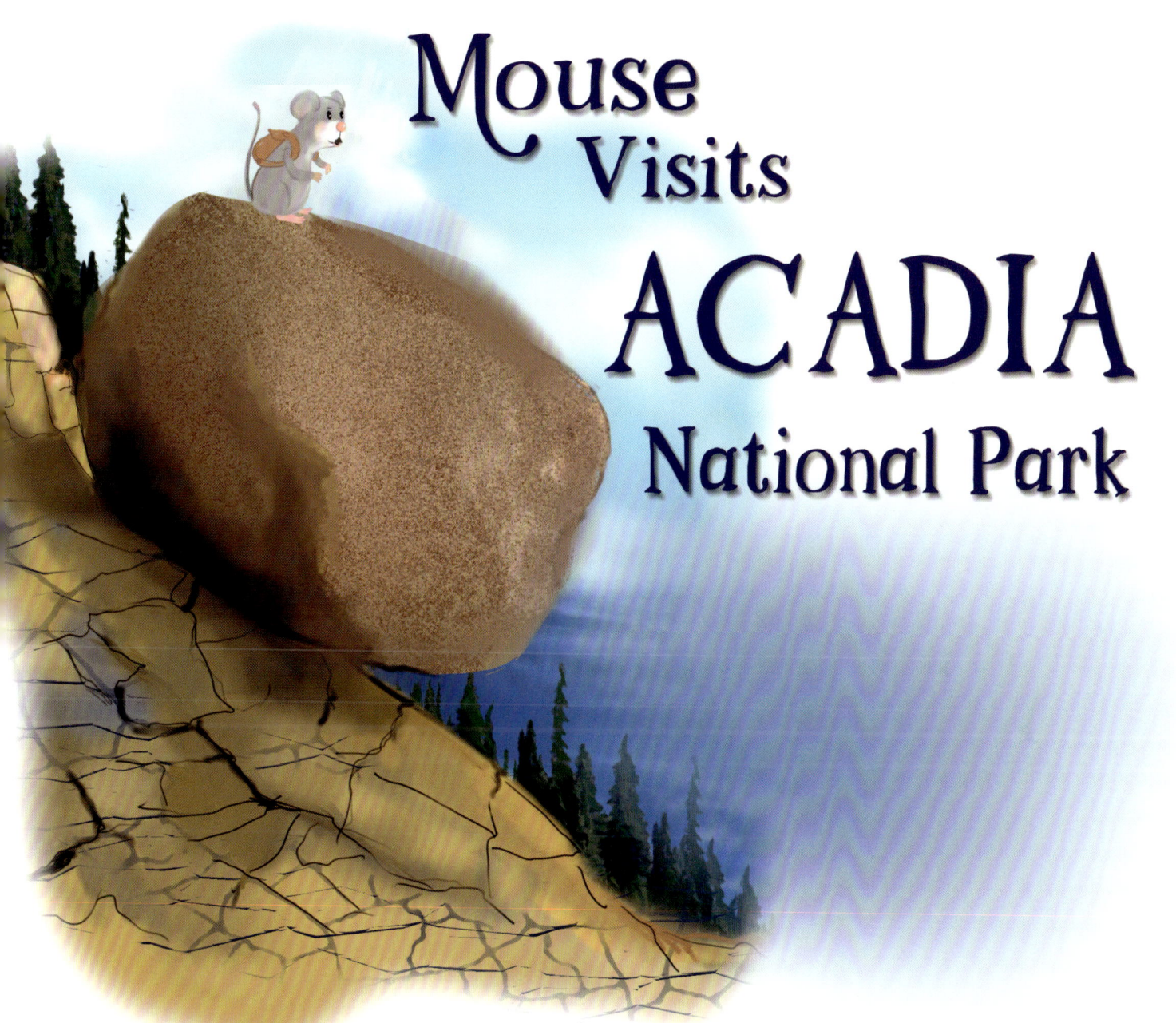

Mouse Visits ACADIA National Park

written by Tricia Gardella
illustrated by Ginger Nielson

To Megan, my favorite water girl. TG
To Leo, who makes each day a bit sweeter.

Mouse Visits Acadia National Park

Copyright Text © Tricia Gardella 2024
Copyright Art © Ginger Nielson 2024
Publisher's Cataloging-in-Publication data
Names: Gardella, Tricia, author. | Nielson, Ginger, illustrator. Title: Mouse visits Acadia National Park / by Tricia Gardella; illustrated by Ginger Nielson.Series: Mouse Traveler Description: Revised edition. | Jamestown, CA: Write 'em Cowgirl, 2023. | Summary: Mouse wakes one morning wanting to see an ocean. Off he goes to find a laptop to jump the letters that will teleport him to Acadia National Park just in time to see the fall colors.Identifiers: ISBN: 9781959412-49-6 | 9781959412502 Subjects: LCSH Mice--Juvenile fiction. | Acadia National Park (Me.)--Juvenile fiction. | Adventure fiction. | BISAC JUVENILE FICTION / Action & Adventure / General
Classification: Classification: LCC PZ7.1 .G37 Mo 2023 | DDC [E]--d

Acadia National Park was established February 26, 1919. It covers 75 square miles.

In what State (states) can Acadia National Park be found?

What other creatures not mentioned in this book might be found in Acadia National Park?

Does Acadia National Park look the same all year?

What differences might different seasons bring?

What is a botanical garden?

How tall is Cadillac Mountain?

What is the purpose of a light house?

One late Fall morning, Mouse woke and decided he wanted to visit an ocean. He knew just the place. He rushed to a computer. It was Saturday. No kids today. He jumped from letter to letter. ACADIA NATIONAL PARK. ENTER. ESC.

Here came the rumble. Everything went black. Whoosh. He felt his body racing. Fast. Then, thump, it stopped, and all was light.

Mouse found himself standing on a flat rock with water all around, back-to-back with a humongous animal. The animal rolled over.

Mouse jumped away. "I'm looking for a mouse," he squeaked.

"That could turn into a real ordeal," barked seal. He turned over and went back to sleep.

Mouse looked around. Waves washed in and out around the rock. The hills gleamed red, orange, yellow and purple. Beneath them he saw a parking lot. That's where he needed to be. As soon as the waves headed out, he scurried across the sand.

Mouse glimpsed a bird perched on a rock.
"I'm looking for mice," he squeaked.
"How dull," screamed Gull, and off he flew.

Mouse noticed a critter moving in a rocky pool. He climbed down.

"Have you seen any mice?" he asked.

"Gab, gab, gab," said Crab. She clicked a claw at Mouse, before scudding into the sea.

Mouse was climbing up to the parking lot when he spotted a deer standing in the middle of the road. He hurried over. "Have you seen any mice?"
"You rarely find them near here," said Deer.

Mouse adjusted the straps on the new backpack he had made and headed for the lot. It seemed forever before he heard a family coming back to their car.

Mouse scrambled up into the engine.

It wasn't long before the car slowed, then stopped. Mouse waited a few minutes before climbing from his hiding place.

Wild Gardens of Acadia, a sign read. Colorful trees spread everywhere along the pathways. It looked to be a perfect place to find mice.

In minutes a tiny nose poked out from under a plant.
"I see you," called Mouse. "Are you the only mouse in the area?"
"I'm a White-Footed Mouse," the mouse announced.
"You look just like my friend, Nosy, and he was a Deer Mouse."

"White-Footed, Deer Mouse, same thing. What are you?"

"I'm a House Mouse," said Mouse.

"I'm Frank. Come on. I'll introduce you to my family." Soon Mouse was surrounded by Frank's cousins. Frank chatted a moment with his family.

"We're taking you to Cadillac Mountain," Frank announced. "We might find more mice there."
"Follow me!" Mouse hollered. The mice looked at each other. Did he know how to get to Cadillac Mountain?

"Come on!" Mouse showed the gang where and how to load into a car. Some of the cousins held back. "You are going to like the time this saves," Mouse promised. Once loaded some of them enjoyed playing tag while motoring along.

The car stopped, they counted to ten. They climbed down. This was not the trail to Cadillac Mountain. A sign said Egg Rock Lighthouse.

"Maybe we can find a boat and go out there," said Frank.

The cousins looked out to sea. They could barely see the lighthouse and the water was choppy.

"Maybe we can save that trip for another day," said Mouse.

The cousins sighed with relief. Riding in a car was enough new for one day. Back into the car they climbed. When the car stopped again. The mice waited their allotted time.

Then they climbed down and began their climb. The view was breathtaking.

Mouse noticed a tree moving ahead.

"Who let you loose?" grumbled Moose, as they neared.

"A moose, a moose, we've never seen a moose," squealed the cousins.

"Around here, they are very rare," agreed Snowshoe Hare, hopping by.

This is the tallest mountain on the Eastern seaboard," one of the cousins announced proudly when they reached the top.

Down the opposite side they stumbled, following a sign for Bubble Rock. As they marched along Mouse asked every animal they passed if they had seen any other mice.

"You'll find some soon," promised Raccoon.
"Mice stink," said Mink.
"I've seen a few here and there," growled Bear.
"Good luck," called Woodchuck.

"Bet I can make you howl," hooted Snowy Owl. He then spread his wings and swooped. Every mouse dove for the nearest hidey hole.

"What is an owl doing out in the daytime?" Frank wondered.

When all was clear, the mice resumed their hike.
It wasn't long before they came to some water.
"We're looking for mice," said Mouse.
"You might find one under this log," croaked Frog.

"Too dank for mice," said Mouse. He turned toward a toothy critter chewing on a nearby tree. "I don't know either," lisped Beaver.

Frank hugged Mouse. "Sorry, but we need to be getting back." The cousins climbed into a car headed homeward.

Mouse chose one he hoped was heading for Bubble Rock.

Yikes. Bubble Rock was a long hike from its parking lot. Mouse felt scared when he climbed on the rock. It seemed like it might fall at any second. Mouse looked out over the ocean.

He was deciding where to go next when, Whooooosh. He felt his body racing. Fast.

Then, thump, he was home. He felt bad that he hadn't seen more of Acadia but there was always next time.

Our National Parks matter!

More than 100 years ago the United States established its first National Park—Yellowstone. The idea was to preserve some of our most beautiful and unique lands to be enjoyed by generations to come. This was at a time when there were a lot of open lands. Not everyone agreed. Many National Parks include hard to find products that can be used by industry. It is up to us and future generations to decide what is more important, products such as lumber for building more houses, or a protected ecosystem where wildlife can feel safe and multiply. National Parks are places where families and tourists can appreciate a few relatively accessible wide- open and unique spaces of our wondrous Earth. Many are centers of learning. Some are mainly for hiking the great outdoors. And some are used by scientists as a measure of climate change. National Parks help to protect natural resources. They are a way to provide clean water, clean air and protect open space for generations to come. But this can only happen if we care enough to take care of them. I have loved National Parks since a time when there were only a few parks— I was a little girl then. Today we have over 60 National Parks in this country alone.

Not only do I now have grandchildren, I have great-grandchildren and I would love them all to have the opportunity to share the wonder of our National treasures with their great-grandchildren, too.

There was a time when Acadia National Park seemed a far-off destination. Today thousands of tourists visit it to celebrate its beauty every year. Unfortunately, population pressures, pollution, invasive animal species and climate change are taking their toll. Our National Park system tells us "Acadia's temperatures are warming, growing seasons are lengthening, we have more precipitation, with bigger storms. Sea level has risen by eight inches since 1950, and the ocean is warmer and more acidic. Invasive animals, pests, diseases, and plants are capitalizing on stressed ecosystems to spread further and deeper, outcompeting native species." How can we help?.

Thank you to Acadia NP Headquarters for giving me direction.